Teddy the Dog

Be Your Own Dog

by Keri Claiborne Boyle
pictures by Jonathan Sneider

HARPER
An Imprint of HarperCollinsPublishers

Teddy the Dog: Be Your Own Dog

Illustrations by Jon Nez based on original sketches by Jonathan Sneider

For information address HarperCollins Children's Books, a division of HarperCollins Publishers, 195 Broadway, New York, NY 10007.
www.harpercollinschildrens.com

ISBN 978-0-06-238283-2

Typography by Jeanne L. Hogle
16 17 18 19 20 SCP 10 9 8 7 6 5 4 3 2 1

First Edition

Even though dogs rule and people drool, I'd still like to give embarrassing sniffs and slobbery face licks to Team Teddy: Jon Sneider, Michelle O'Brien, Ted Pidcock, Keri Claiborne Boyle, Erica Antonio, Betsy Wegman, Richard Curbello, Jessimara Martins, & Honey the Dog. Laughter (and fur babies) make the world go 'round.
—Teddy the Dog

To Andrew, Riley, Kayleigh too, and li'l Nolan . . . my family zoo
—Keri Claiborne Boyle

For my family—Mindy, Cary, Jeff, Jordan, & Honey the Dog
—Jonathan Sneider

Folks, life is *great* here in Teddy-ville.

RED'S MEAT SHOP

I'm the leader of the pack. The big cheese.

Top dog, one might even say.

I'm a charming and fetching dog.

Who never *actually* fetches.

I'm happy just living by my own simple motto . . .

Be your own dog.

I'm also *quite* helpful. How, you ask? Well . . .

The neighbors just can't get enough of all the sweet lullabies I sing at night.

And I've been known to bring business to the local food cart.

I always give the neighborhood house painter a helping paw.

You know, all those things that make me so doggone lovable.

I mean, who *else* would get anywhere near your sweaty socks?

And that's *exactly* why it nearly blew
the fleas right off my tail when one day,
completely unannounced . . .

a large and *very* mysterious-looking package showed up.

Dearest Teddy,
Please take care of
sweet little Penelope.
Love,
Aunt Marge

CATas

trophe!

Couldn't you just let a sleeping dog lie? Why add a cat when you already have a perfectly good dog?

Worst of all? The box didn't come with return postage. How was I supposed to send it back?

And even *more* worst of all? I couldn't write a letter of complaint. I don't have thumbs!

I quickly realized I was stuck with this unexpected arrival like a burr in my fur. Like it or not, this cat was here to stay.

But I guess when life gives you a mud puddle, you just have to roll in it. Right?

So I decided to make the best of it and teach little Fishbreath a thing or two about living a dog's life.

You know, help her fit in . . . Teddy-style.

First, I tried to show Fishbreath how to have some fun. But it turns out cats don't do the doggie paddle.

And windblown is definitely *not* a good look for her . . .

Then I tried to teach her how to act like the king of the house. But her idea of barking could use a little improvement. And she seemed reluctant to chase suspicious cars.

But just when I was about to give up,
we did find *one* thing we could agree on . . .

neither of us is ever going to fetch. It was looking like this was going to be a "No Fetching" friendship.

I realized Fishbreath wasn't so bad after all. Maybe it was time to throw her a bone and try something different.

Perhaps she could even teach this (remarkably cute) dog some new tricks!

But there are some things a dog is just not supposed to do.

And her idea of fun was like staring at a broken TV.

While I'm not a scaredy-cat, other things would definitely end badly.

It was all turning out to be harder than I thought. I was starting to wonder if there was *anything* we had in common.

Maybe Fishbreath has the right idea. . . .

A catnap *would* do a doggie some good.

Perhaps we're not so different after all . . . Fishbreath and me.

I guess we're both trying to be who we're meant to be.

Because you just gotta be your own dog . . .

. . . even if it means being a cat.